Acknowledgements

There are so many people that I would like to extend my thanks to that I cannot possibly fit them all in here. But I hope that if they all squish up a bit, there will be room for as many as possible. So, without further ado my thanks to: my amazing parents, for encouraging me to write and publish this book. I would like to thank my little brothers, Aadi and Shri for giving me a few ideas for my book and being my brothers in general. Thank you so much to my grandparents (Jejema, Babba, Naani) for guiding me all through.

A special thank you to all my teachers at Invergowrie Primary School, who have taught me how to spell, read, write, and learn so much more. A special mention to Mrs. Glenn for reviewing and editing even with her busy schedule. Thanks to all my friends, for keeping me company, and never leaving me alone. Thanks to my favourite authors, J.K Rowling, Sophie Cleverly, Jaqueline Wilson, Natasha Farrant, Lemony Snicket, Kathrine Rundell, Enid Blyton, Stephenie Meyer, Roald Dahl, Pamela Butchart and Jennifer Killick for inspiring me to write.

There are others who have helped this book on its way some way or another, providing love and support, or just being there to prevent writing-related meltdowns. To name a few; my cousins, aunts and uncles, and, of course the rest of my family.

Finally, thank you for reading. Hillton School will be keeping its doors open, just for you...

In loving memory of Jejebapa (my grandpa) and Bhengi jejebapa ... we miss you!

EMMELINE GREY AND THE GREAT ADVENTURE

by

Shona Nanda

CHAPTER 1- THE BEGINNING

One morning 12-year-old Emmeline Grey was woken up by her alarm. She gazed out of the window of Hillton's Boarding school for boys and girls. It was another cold, grey winter day, but it was her birthday, so she was very excited. She looked around the dormitory. It was deserted, so Emily guessed the others have gone down for breakfast. She woke up Poppy (her puppy), dressed into her school uniform (a white shirt with a collar, a blue and bronze tie, a blue skirt and a blue blazer with the school crest on it). She looked around the dormitory again. It was decorated with blue and bronze bunting and blue banners which said, 'Happy Birthday!' on them. Under all the second years' beds were presents. Emily ran to each bed excitedly, ripping open all the presents her friends had given her (all the beds had presents under them except Mia Foxglove, Max Foxglove and James Frarrant's beds). She got a big box of sweets from Rachel Taylor, a luxury eagle quill from Lily Thomas, a new collar for Poppy embroidered with Poppy's from Charlie Duncan and a make-up set from Felicity Duncan. Emily combed her hair, put the new collar on Poppy, put some make up on, grabbed her blue school bag with all her things she would need for her lessons that day along with her timetable, and rushed down the stairs into the second-year common room. Mia was in there, playing a game on her tablet. She looked up at Emily, pulled a face at her, and carried on playing. She looked at the time on her phone Miss Nott had given her (Miss Nott had volunteered to look after Emily after her parents died when she was a baby). It was 8:00 am. She dashed out of the common room, and into the deserted corridor. She could hear noises from the Great Hall. She ran into it and, panting, sat between Rachel and Charlie. 'Happy birthday Emily, did you like our presents?' asked Lily. 'Yeah, they were really nice, thanks,' said Emily, helping herself to some bacon, eggs, sausages and toast. 'I see you're wearing the make up I gave you,' said Felicity, smiling. Charlie looked at Poppy's collar and grinned. 'You've put Poppy's new collar on her too' he said, stroking Poppy's soft white fur gently. She barked happily back at him. Charlie had soft blonde hair and had bright blue eyes, just like his older sister, Felicity. Lily was brown haired and a little tanned with bright green eyes. Rachel had white-blonde hair and blue-green eyes, and Emily had freckles, curly red hair, braces and deep brown eyes. 'Have you eaten any of the sweets I gave you yet?' asked Rachel eagerly. 'No, not yet,' replied Emily, munching on her toast. 'But I will,' she added quickly. Rachel smiled at her. 'Hope you enjoy them. I made sure to buy all your favourite sweets,' said Rachel enthusiastically. 'I'm going to use my new quill in all my lessons,' said Emily excitedly, pouring herself some juice. 'I never knew I'd have such good friends like you,' she continued, making her glass of juice overflow. 'Oops,' she said, as the juice soaked the end of the sleeves of her blazer.

Rachel, Lily, Charlie, Felicity and Emily burst into gales of laughter until at last Emily stood up to get some paper towels to mop up the juice. Lily helped and Rachel poured her a new glass of juice. After, they went back into the common room before their first lesson, which was Botany. They watched Lily and Emily do TikToks together before heading to the greenhouses with the fourth years. Botany was taught by Professor Carrots. She suited her name very well. She had carrot- coloured hair and deep blue eyes.

'Today we will be growing tomato or potato plants. These will be helpful for the cooks as they are cooking leek and potato soup in six months, and potatoes grow usually around six months time. If they don't, don't worry because the year sevens and year fives planted them last month. Now, fourth years, come and pick which seeds you want to plant!' she said, and the fourth years rushed forward and most of them chose tomato seeds. There were only 3 tomato seeds left. 'Now, second years, come and choose seeds. No pushing!' Professor Carrots said, as two boys came rushing forward to grab the tomato seeds with all the rest of the second years following behind. Rachel grabbed them first. 'Here Emily, take it. ' Emily shook her head. 'You got it; you take it Rachel.' 'No, have it, I actually want potato seeds,' said Rachel, shoving the seeds into Emily's hands. Emily nodded her head slowly. 'Professor, Grey got the last tomato seeds,' moaned Mia. 'Well, I haven't got any more, do I Mia? Professor Carrots replied. ' Everyone likes stupid brace-face,' Mia muttered to Max and James as she walked up to them with her potato seeds. They sniggered. Mia smirked. 'Hey, Emily, I forgot to say happy birthday to you!' Said Professor Carrots. Emily grinned up at her. 'Oh, and I don't think those are enough seeds,' Professor Carrots added, looking at Emily's palm. 'Don't tell Mia, but I have spare seeds. 'She took about seven more seeds out of her pocket and gave them to her. Emily took them, and Professor Carrots smiled and winked at her kindly. Emily couldn't help but smile back. Then she hurried back to Lily. 'She actually had spare seeds!' she told Lily excitedly. 'But she told Mia she didn't!' said Charlie, shaking soil out of his hair. 'How did you get soil in your hair?' Emily asked Charlie. 'Oh, James pin-head threw it at my head,' and before anyone could stop him, he picked up two big fistfuls of soil and hurled the soil at James. It hit him right on the back of the head, and he turned round and tried to punch Charlie, who was laughing. Still sniggering, he ducked the punch and James ended punching a fourth year boy with brown hair, who ended up having to go to the hospital wing. Charlie turned around and smirked. None of them laughed and Felicity raised her eyebrows at Charlie, but for the rest of the class Charlie was serious. When they had planted and watered their plants, they went back to the castle for their next and least favourite lesson-Science with the first years. As they headed towards the science classroom, they heard someone following them. It was Max. Suddenly their science teacher, Professor Facts, appeared in front of them. He had oily blond hair and dull grey eyes. 'In,' He said, in his very oily voice. 'You're 10 minutes late. Detention for you all except Mr. Foxglove, of course. It is not his fault that he is late, it is yours. 'He smiled his thin, icy smile, and beckoned them into his classroom. They entered. Max went to sit next to Mia, and Lily, Rachel, Charlie, Felicity and Emily got a table to themselves. Emily saw Max give something to Mia, who smirked when she took the thing Max had. Emily prodded Rachel on the shoulder and pointed at Max, James and Mia, who were giggling and writing on their exercise books. Before Rachel could say anything, Professor Facts said, 'Today we will be experimenting on chemical explosions.' 'That's very interesting, Professor,' said James. 'Yes, it certainly is interesting, Mr. Frarrant.' said Professor Facts. Lily rolled her eyes. 'Right. Let's get started, shall we? Lab coats, safety goggles and gloves on!' The class silently and obediently pulled on their gloves, goggles and lab coats. When they had all put their things on, Professor Facts said 'Now, for the first experiment you will need your bicarbonate of soda and red food colouring from your kit. I will give you half a lemon, washing up liquid and a narrow glass.' He handed out half a lemon, a large tub of washing up liquid and a long, narrow glass. 'First, put a teaspoon of bicarbonate of soda into the glass,' He instructed the class.

The class followed his instructions. 'Stir in a squirt of washing up liquid, then add two drops of food colouring.' again, the glass followed Professor Facts' instructions. 'Lastly, add in all the lemon juice that you have,' the class squirted the lemon juice into their glasses. The contents of Emily's glass fizzed and exploded perfectly. Charlie ripped a piece of paper out from his exercise book and scribbled something on it, then he handed it to Emily under the table. It said How do you do that?! Look at mine! Emily glanced at Charlie's glass. Inside was a puss coloured liquid, which was bubbling furiously. She ripped a piece of paper out of her exercise book and wrote back 'I think you added too much washing up liquid and baking soda' and handed it to Charlie, who scribbled Alright, thanks! Next time we do this experiment (which is probably going to be in like 2 months' time) I'll keep that in mind! Hey, want to go for a swim in the pool after lunch? How about going fishing in the lake? Last time I went to the lake, guess what I saw? A big, fat salmon! Isn't that amazing? If we do go fishing, I wonder if we'll see that salmon again? Imagine if I caught it? THAT WOULD BE AWESOME! Anyway, enough about that, but please, please, please can we go fishing in the lake? And handed it back to Emily. She wrote back in a hurry You're welcome and sure we can go fishing, but we **_can't talk now_** because if Professor Facts sees us, we're going to get double detention! She handed it back to Charlie, who nodded and slipped the piece of paper into his pocket. Luckily, Professor Facts didn't see them because he was too busy helping Mia, who's explosion didn't work. When he was done, he stood up and went back to the front of the class. Then he said, ' Now we will be doing a different type. Keep the washing up liquid and the narrow glass but give the lemons back to me. I will also be giving out cocktail style glasses and vinegar for the next experiment.' He went around the class, taking the lemons and handing out cocktail style glasses and vinegar. 'Now, let's get started. Miss Millan, we are using the same things included in our kit, 'Professor Facts said, as a girl called Louise Millan put her food colouring into her bag. She turned an interesting shade of puce and took the food colouring back out. 'First of all, put a teaspoon of bicarbonate of soda into the glass, then cover it with water.' The class put a teaspoon of bicarbonate of soda and took out their water bottles and poured water into the glass until it was filled to the brim. 'Now add two drops of food colouring, then add in a splash of vinegar.' The class followed his instructions. Once again, the contents of Emily's glass fizzed and exploded neatly. This time, Charlie's worked too. Emily ripped a small piece of a page out of her exercise book

and wrote; Well done, Charlie! and handed it to Charlie. Charlie grinned and wrote back Thanks! Can't wait to go fishing! and handed it back to Emily. 'Now, who can tell me what is happening in this experiment?' said Professor Facts. Felicity raised her hand. 'Mr. Farrant, do you know?' Professor Facts asked. 'Nope, 'answered James. 'OK. No one else? Alright, I will tell you. So...'Please Professor, I know!' said Felicity. 'The bicarbonate of soda reacts with the citric acid in the lemon in experiment 1 and with the acetic acid in the vinegar in experiment 2 to form carbon dioxide gas filled expanding fizzy bub-' **'<u>SILENCE!</u>'** bellowed professor Facts. '-bles' Felicity finished silently.

'So, as I was saying before I was most *rudely* interrupted, 'he glared at Felicity, 'I will tell you. Well I would, but what Miss Duncan has said is correct. You all may go for lunch now. You're five minutes late for lunch. NOW GO!' The class grabbed their bags and stuffed their food colouring, lab coats and everything else into their bags and ran out of the class. Suspiciously, Mia, Max and James hurried ahead of all the first and second years. When Rachel, Lily, Emily, Charlie and Felicity had got to the common room to put their bags into their lockers, Mia was already going out, looking strangely satisfied. When Emily opened her locker, she found three notes inside. The first one said *Hi Emily. Felicity here. I just wanted to say that I don't want to be your friend anymore (and neither does Charlie), because we think you are very stupid and bad at maths. Usually I would say 'from your best Friend, Felicity Duncan', but I'm not your friend anymore. From your ex-friend, Felicity Duncan.* The second one said HELLO EMILY, ME AND RACHEL DO NOT WANT TO BE YOUR FRIEND ANYMORE BECAUSE YOU ARE BRAINLESS. SINCERELY, LILY (AND RACHEL) P.S. WE ARE NOW FRIENDS WITH MIA, JAMES AND MAX. And the last one said Yup, wee hav desided that wee ar not going too bee yor frend any mor so huh! Emily smiled. 'Way to spell, Max,' she said calmly, crumpling the pieces of paper and chucking them into the fire. Mia, Max and James were watching Emily to see her reaction, and when she looked at them, they were all staring at her with dropped jaws. Emily shoved her bag into her locker and walked out of the door towards The Great Hall. She sat down beside Rachel and began to fill her plate with beef, roast potato and yorkshire pudding. After lunch, Lily, Rachel, Felicity, Charlie and Emily went back to the common room to get their bags. There was half an hour left until their next lesson, which was history, so Emily sat down and started to read the news on her phone. Suddenly, Emily froze. 'Are you OK, Emily?' asked Rachel nervously. Emily handed her the phone. Lily, Rachel, Charlie and Felicity read it, and Felicity put the video on. Everyone in the common room stopped what they were doing to listen to it. The news reporter sounded very worried indeed. 'All schools (including boarding schools) are closing. All trains and buses are cancelled, and any cars seen on the streets, the driver will be fined £80 because there is a dangerous criminal named The Baron is on the loose. If the Baron is caught, then everything shall open again. Goodbye!' Emily put her phone back into her pocket and everyone in the common room resumed what they were doing. 'Why do we need to leave school?' moaned a second year called Matthew Lewis. Just then, like a dam bursting, all the second years that were anywhere else in the castle burst into the common room, followed by Professor McCloud, the History teacher. She ran into the room, her black as coal hair flying behind her. 'Pack up your trunks, school is closing down, we just read the news in the staff room,' she said in her Scottish accent. The second years nodded and went to the second-year dormitory to pack their trunks. Emily packed her trunk, went to the Animal House to get Poppy, who was playing with a kitten with black fur. She picked Poppy and the kitten up and went to the sixth-year common room to give the cat to its owner who was a girl called Penelope Peters. She knocked on the door and it was opened by Professor Gabrielle, the language teacher. 'Yes?' she asked in her Italian accent. 'I was wondering if I could give this cat to Penny,' replied Emily. 'Of course, you can! Miss. Penelope?' said Professor Gabrielle. A tall girl with short and wavy blonde hair appeared at the staircase. 'Yes, professor? I'm in the middle of packing, 'said Penelope. 'Yes, sorry to bother you, but Miss Emmeline here would like to give you your cat,' said Professor Gabrielle. 'Oh, naughty Shadow, I was looking all over the castle for you! Thanks, Em!' said Penelope, rushing down the stairs and taking Shadow from Emily. 'You're welcome, Penny,' said Emily. She left the sixth-year common room and went back to the second-year common room. Outside the common room there was a note in Felicity's handwriting. It said: Hello Emily, we have gone to the train station to wait for the train to arrive. When you come back, you will find that there is a lock on the common room door. Emily looked at the door which had a lock on it So you cannot go into the dorm to get your trunk but don't worry, because I knew you wouldn't make it back in time to get to the train station with us, so I got it and, I have it, so when you come to the train station I will give it to you. From Felicity. xxx Emily ran down a corridor, went down a staircase turned a corner, went down another staircase and down another corridor until finally she got to the enormous oak doors of the castle and pushed her way through the crowd of eleventh years, past the lake and football field, down a path and into the train station where there was a large crowd of the school pupils. Emily stood on a large rock and saw Felicity waving at her. Emily waved back and pushed through the crowd of people until she got to Felicity. 'Here's your trunk,' said Felicity handing Emily's trunk to her. Emily took the trunk and said, 'Thanks Felicity.' 'You're welcome, it was nothing really, but your trunk *was* pretty heavy. Well, I did get some help from Charlie,' said Felicity, smiling kindly. Emily smiled widely back at her. She stood on her toes and looked over the top of all the heads of the students and saw a blue and bronze snake coming towards the station. It was the train. Emily nudged Felicity and pointed at it. Felicity watched the train as it pulled into the station. As soon as the doors opened, the first years rushed forward to get into the train. 'Bunch of scaredy-cats,' whispered Mia to Max. He giggled and said 'Yeah, scaredy-cats'. James had also heard what they had said. 'Scaredy-cats, scaredy-cats, scaredy-cats,' he taunted. Once all the first years had got into the train, it was the second years' turn. After the second years had went in, the third years went in, and it continued like that, year after year, until the whole school was in the train, and after all the students had got into the train, the teachers went in. The trains doors closed, and it started to move. Lily, Felicity, Rachel, Charlie and Emily got a compartment to themselves. Poppy started barking loudly. 'It's alright Poppy, we're going home!' said Emily, stroking Poppy. After about fifteen minutes, Poppy fell asleep. 'Whew! Finally! She's gone to sleep!' said Felicity. A Lady with a trolley full of snacks came bustling over.

'Anything from the trolley?' she asked Lily, who usually bought almost everything on the trolley. 'Yes please!' said Lily. 'Can we have... hmm.....how about a jumbo pack of crisps! And Haribos! Ooh, ooh, and Malteser bars! And.....her list went on and on. 'Have any of those?' the lady took out all of the treats and said 'Yes, we do Lilyanna'. That will be £10.50 please,' Lily took out her purse and a £10.00 note and a 50p coin. 'Here you go,' she said, handing the money to the lady. 'Thank you, Lilyanna!' said the lady, Mrs. Milton. Lily ripped open the bag of crisps. Mrs. Milton smiled and walked off. Charlie picked up a remote, 'I really wish she wouldn't call me my stupid name; I really hate it.' mumbled Lily, wrinkling her nose. 'Don't say that! it's lovely! It's named after one of the prettiest flowers in the whole world!' said Felicity, shocked. 'Yeah, I agree with Felicity, I love Lily's,' said Emily. 'Yeah, but Lily's much better than Lilyanna!' 'It's not stupid!' said Felicity angrily, 'Of course, it is!' 'No! it's lovely!' said Emily. 'You mean it's horrible,' muttered Lily. Charlie wanted to change the subject, so he said, 'What do you want to watch?' Emily, Lily and Felicity stopped arguing and Emily said 'Twilight, Breaking Dawn-Part 1.' 'I love that movie! Let's watch that!', said Lily. 'But there are so many other movies to choose from, like The Titanic, Harry Potter, Wonder, Zombies, Descendants, The Parent Trap, Dolphin Tale, The Curse of the Nun, Creep- 'don't start listing horror movies now! 'said Felicity. 'Anyway, my favourite bit of Twilight is when-' 'Ok, Ok, don't ruin the movie for me! I've never watched it before!' interrupted Rachel. 'Ok, but I'm sure you'll love

15

Twilight!', said Lily. Charlie turned on the movie. It was two hours long, and by the time the movie was finished, they had arrived at Verdicts Train Station. 'You were right Lily, that movie was good,' said Rachel excitedly when they had got off the train. 'I know, it's really good, isn't it?' replied Lily. 'Yep, one of my favourite movies,' said Emily, looking around the train station. 'What are you looking for?' asked Felicity. 'I'm looking for Miss Nott's limo, 'answered Emily. After a while she spotted Miss Nott's limo parked in the station, then saw Miss Nott coming out of it. 'Oh, Miss Nott has come. See you some time, 'said Emily sadly, taking Miss Nott's hand and walking off. 'See you, 'said Felicity, Charlie, Lily and Rachel together, and they all set off in different directions. Emily climbed into Miss Nott's limo and Miss Nott told the chauffer to get them home as soon as possible. Once they had got to Miss Nott's house, it was dinner time. They had sausages and mash for dinner and chocolate cake for pudding. Emily was sleepy, so she dressed into her pajamas, brushed her teeth, got a present from Miss Nott (an iPod with earplugs) and then went to bed. She soon fell asleep. At exactly midnight, someone poked her hard. She sat up in her bed. She looked around. It was Lily. Emily jumped. 'It's only me, silly!' said Lily, laughing. 'Yeah, I know, but how did you get here?' she asked, startled. She must have said it a bit too loud, because it woke up Miss Nott. Emily heard footsteps outside her door. 'Quick, hide under here!' hissed Emily hurriedly, yanking her bed sheet up and pointing to the trapdoor where they held all their secret meetings. Lily opened it and didn't even bother to use the ladder. She just jumped through the door and landed with a thud on the wooden floor of the small room. Emily shut the door and sat back down in her bed just in time. Miss Nott came into the room. 'Are you Ok?' she asked in her strong French accent. 'Yeah, yeah I'm fine,' replied Emily, as innocently as possible. 'I thought I heard you talking to someone. It must be my imagination. Why are you awake? 'Miss Nott continued. *Uh Oh,* thought Emily, *I'm dead meat.* She thought fast. 'I thought I heard a…um…a…bird, so I…so I wanted to take a…photo of it,' said Emily, pulling out her phone and showed a random photo of a bird in school she had taken when they were planting flowers in botany. 'Ooh, zat iz very nice. Iz it Ok if you send zat picture to me?' said Miss Nott. 'Yes, of course I can,' replied Emily sweetly. 'Thank you very much, Emily,' said Miss Nott kindly. Emily smiled, and Miss Nott left the room. Emily opened the trapdoor and climbed down the ladder. Inside, Lily was sitting on the old mattress they used as a sofa.

CHAPTER 2- LILY'S PLAN

'So, how did you get here?' asked Emily, when they were wrapped up in blankets and had mugs of hot chocolate (Lily had to change into spare clothes she had brought). ' Easy! I walked here,' said Lily 'and I sprained my ankle on the way,' she added, showing Emily her black ankle. Emily looked worried. 'Don't worry, I'm fine. It doesn't even hurt!' the expression on Emily's face calmed down a bit. 'Oh, and how did you get up to my bedroom? It's on the sixth floor!' exclaimed Emily. 'There's a pipe on the side of your bedroom. I simply climbed up it. I-' 'How on earth did you climb the pipe? It's raining outside and the pipe is really slippery!' 'Um...I put chalk on my hands to help me grip the pipe. Still, it was really hard to climb that pipe!' 'Ok, so why did you come here?' 'Please can you just shut up?' 'Yeah, ok,' said Emily. Lily jumped up, spilling her mug of hot chocolate. Emily wondered what on earth she was trying to do. Before Emily could ask her, she was already in Emily's room. A few minutes later, Lily came back with a small sack. She opened it and tipped it upside down. A piece of rolled up paper, a letter addressed to Felicity and Charlie and a printout of a recipe came out. Lily unrolled the piece of paper and showed it to Emily. It was a map. ' I copied it off google. I want to catch The Baron. 'Emily knew she would be yelled at by Lily again if she spoke, so she kept quiet and nodded. Then she realized what Lily was saying. 'Wait, what?' she said. 'I want to catch The Baron.' Lily repeated. 'No way! How are we supposed to do that?' Emily said. 'Just listen to me first, will you?' said Lily in mock puzzlement. 'Oh yeah, 'said Emily sarcastically. 'So basically, I found three suspicious places where the Baron could be hiding. Number one: the mountains beside our school. Next to Hillton Village, remember?' Emily nodded. 'Number two: Megahurtz Lake. That's beside our school too. And number three: an unknown place beside Megahurtz lake. I reckon it's the third one because 1-whoever's tried to get in there has never managed to make it out alive, and: 2-nobody knows that place's name, so we're going there.' 'But how the hell are we going to get there? 'Emily just couldn't keep quiet. 'Whoever's got in there's never got out, and it's near school! It'll take us weeks, never mind days, because all the trains are cancelled!' 'Don't worry about that right now. I'll tell you the rest of the plan later,' said Lily calmly. 'I've written a letter to Felicity and Charlie. Here, read it , 'it said: Hey Fliss, Charles, this is a short and URGENT letter. I'll explain it more when you guys COME OVER TO MISS NOTT'S HOUSE AS SOON AS YOU CAN. Don't take your time, pack your bag, don't tell your parents about this and DON'T BRING A SUITCASE please. If you take your time, I will yell at you for 1000 years and call you... something bad for the rest of your life. Love from Lil xxx P.S just want to tell you how to get to 'Miss Nott's house. Put chalk on your hands and climb up the pipe beside Em's bedroom window. 'I think you should change the 'if you take your time, I will yell at you for 1000 years, and call you... something bad, for the rest of your life, 'part, it sounds a bit rude,' said Emily. Lily nodded, grabbed a quill and an ink bottle and scribbled on the piece of paper. When Emily looked at it again, instead of *if you take your time, I will yell at you for 1000 years and call you... something bad for the rest of your life* it said *if you take your time, I will yell at you for 1000 years!* ~~and call you... something bad for the rest of your life.~~ 'Better than last time, I suppose,' said Emily.

'Now you write yours,' said Lily, handing a piece of paper, Emily's eagle quill and a bottle of ink to Emily. Emily dipped the quill into the ink and began writing her letter to Rachel. *Hello Rachel, this is a short letter. But it's URGENT. Come to Miss Nott's ASAP. Pack a bag, (DON'T BRING A SUITCASE) and do not tell your parents about this, Rachel, please? The reason why you need to come along is because* ~~me and Lily are going to come up with a plan to catch the baron.~~ *Lily has come up with a plan to catch the Baron. Hope to see you soon, Emily. xxx P.S don' t come through the door because the doorman will send you back home. Put chalk on your hands and climb up the pipe beside my bedroom.* She put it in an envelope, then gave it to Lily. Lily took it from her, put the two letters in her pocket, then ran up to the ladder as fast as she could and leaped. She managed to grab hold of the floor above her and kicked the ladder hard and it toppled over and landed with an almighty crash on the floor. Emily thought Miss Nott had woken up, but luckily, she hadn't. When Emily looked up at where Lily was, all she saw was a small note taped to the ladder on the floor. She went over to it and read the note. *Em, went to deliver letters.*

I'm using two things: junk drawer and Poppy. Lil. xxx

What did Lily mean? Oh well, she'd need to ask her when Lily came back. Meanwhile, Lily opened Emily's junk drawer. Inside there was a large nail, a hammer, a rope and a bucket. Suddenly, she had an idea. The window was open, so she climbed onto the windowsill and slowly leaned out of it. It was very cold outside, and Lily started to shiver violently. Nevertheless, she used the hammer to hammer the nail halfway into the wall, picked up the rope and wound it round the nail, then pulled it as hard as she could. Next, she tied the other end of the rope to the bucket, before picking Poppy up and putting her inside the bucket. 'Here, now you can deliver our letters, just like in Harry Potter!' said Lily, lowering Poppy down to the ground. Poppy started barking insanely. 'Please calm down, Poppy! You'll wake everyone in the whole of London up! And can you deliver these two to Rachel and Felicity and Charlie?' Poppy nodded and walked off into the night. About ten minutes later, Poppy came running back to the house with three letters in her mouth. She jumped into the bucket and Lily pulled the rope until the bucket was in line with the windowsill. Lily took the letters from Poppy and picked Poppy up. Almost immediately, Poppy fell asleep. Lily placed Poppy on the bed and went back into their 'Secret Meeting Room'. She sat down beside Emily and opened the first letter. It said Hello Lily , this is so confusing! How on earth can I come to Miss Nott's when the Baron's around? Me and Charlie could get murdered! Charlie insisted that we should go. Why do we even need to come? From Felicity. xxx P.S I guess you have a point about getting to Miss Nott's house safely. If you can do it, why not me and Charlie? Well, I've decided that I will come. Also, is Rachel coming along? The next one said Hey Lily, of course we are going to come to Miss Nott's house! Felicity said "no, we can't go, it's too dangerous!" but I reckon we should go! She's a total wimp. Anyway, I guess she does have a point... It's dangerous to go to other people's houses right now cause the Baron's is on the loose. But just because Felicity's the *older sister,* doesn't mean she can boss *me* about! See you soon, Charlie. xxx P.S Is Rachel coming? and the third one said *Hello Emily, why on earth do I need to come? It's sooo dangerous to go to your house right now at this time of night, especially at these times, with the Baron and his gang running about! Have you heard on the news? There were about 10 more murders in a night! And why don't we just leave the 'catching the Baron stuff' to the police? They've solved loads of difficult mysteries, you know. But.... I guess none of them are as bad as this one...... Anyway, I think I'll tag along. Love from Rachel. x P.S. Is Felicity coming over too?* 'Right, ok, so everyone's coming over. Brilliant!' said Lily, once her and Emily had finished reading the letters. Emily cleared her throat. ' What?' asked Lily. ' I think you've forgotten something,' replied Emily. 'Oh, yeah, I need to tell you the plan!' Lily realized. 'Mm hm,' said Emily, nodding. 'So, basically, we've already done step one of the plan,' said Lily. ' and that was writing the letters to Felicity, Charlie and Rachel. Now step two is: we make a kind of drink that'll keep us warm,' ' What for?'

asked Emily. 'Listen to me and let me tell you the rest of the plan. You've interrupted me twice now,' said Lily. 'I'm so sorry, Lily. Carry on,' muttered Emily. Lily looked as if she had suddenly realized something. She took a piece of paper and one of Emily's quills with a bottle of ink and began to write. Emily read what Lily was writing. It looked like a letter to...Felicity and Charlie? Hello Fliss, Charles, this is urgent. Will answer your Q's when you arrive. Love from Lil. xxx P.S yes, Rach's coming. Em sent a letter to her. Said she'll 'tag along'. P.S. good luck on coming here. I was scared to go to Miss Nott's at this time of night. Especially because of the BARON. Lily folded the piece of paper up and popped it into an envelope. Emily decided she would write one as well. Hi Rachel, I'll answer your questions in this letter. Well, yeah, I did hear the news about the baron running about and killing the Rocher family. I didn't really know them, so don't ask why they were, you know, murdered. You need to come because we want you to help us catching the Baron. You should probably ask Lily about why we shouldn't leave the 'catching the baron stuff" to the police. We're NOT leaving the "catching the baron stuff " to the police because they're complete DUMMIES compared to us. and we'll never get back to school in time for Christmas, Rach. Love, Lil. And lastly, yes, Felicity and Charlie are coming. Love, Emily. xxx She gave her letter to Lily, and Lily gave it to Poppy and lowered her down to the ground in the bucket, then told her to give the letters to Felicity, Charlie and Rachel. Five minutes later, Poppy was back with two letters in her mouth. Lily pulled the rope and poppy leaped into the room before falling asleep again on the bed. Lily took the envelopes and went back inside their secret room. She flopped herself down onto the mattress and opened the envelopes. Inside one were two very small notes. The first one was in Charlie's handwriting and it said Ok and the second one (which was in Felicity's handwriting) said *Hello Lily, yes that's good that Rachel's coming, and I look forward to getting to know what on earth is going on. From Felicity. xxx P.S I've already packed my bag! Just putting my raincoat on, it's raining hard, isn't it?* 'Sure,' said Lily. Emily read Rachel's.

That's fine, Emily. Rachel. x 'So, now can you tell me' ' The rest of the plan,' finished Lily. 'Yeah, I can do that. So, this is how to make the drink. We need...ginger, honey, boiled water, teabags-' ' I'm really sorry to interrupt you again, but how many teabags to we need?' ' Maybe...about nine?' *'Nine? Isn't that a bit too....much?'* 'Nope, we need it like that, so it'll keep us warm. Anyway, we also need...pepper. That's it.' 'So, where do you want to make it?' ' In your kitchen, where else do you think?' 'Ok, I guess that works.' Lily and Emily stood up and climbed up the ladder. They sneaked into the kitchen, then gathered all the ingredients they would need to make the drink. They boiled the water, grated the ginger, added the honey along with the ginger, dropped in all nine of the teabags in together and finally added the pepper in. Soon it was ready. They had made a very big batch of it. They found five giant flasks and poured every drop of the drink into them, before shutting them tightly so none of the heat could escape from the flasks. They sneaked back into their secret room and Lily went home for little while to pack. While she was away, Felicity and Charlie arrived. 'We got the note! Wait...Where's Lily?' said Charlie. 'She's gone home to pack,' said Emily. 'Ok, and where's Rachel?' 'She's not arrived yet,' replied Emily. ' Do any of you want...tea or hot chocolate?' ' Yes please,' said Charlie. 'Can I have some tea, please?' asked Felicity. 'Hot chocolate for me,' said Charlie, and yawned. 'Have you packed yet, Emily?' asked Felicity. 'No, not yet,' answered Emily. About 10 minutes later, Lily came rushing in, panting like a dog. ' Lily, can I have your rucksack for a minute?' asked Felicity. 'Sure, why?' asked Lily, looked puzzled. Felicity just smiled and said, 'You'll see,' Lily, looking quizzical, handed her rucksack to Felicity and Felicity opened it. She took out Lily's quill, ink bottle and a piece of paper. She looked inside Lily's rucksack and began to write. ' What are you doing?' asked Lily curiously. Felicity just continued to write. She wrote for about 5 minutes before giving the piece of paper to Lily. Lily read it and said, 'What's this for?' Emily read it. It said *Things Lily's taking to the trip that we're going on:*

- ❖ *Paper plates*
- ❖ *Paper cups*
- ❖ *A drink to keep us warm*
- ❖ *A sleeping bag*
- ❖ *A torch*
- ❖ *a box of matches*

- ❖ A bottle of water

- ❖ a big loaf of bread

- ❖ A tub of Nutella

- ❖ A tub of butter with an ice pack attached to it

- ❖ Five spare ice packs

- ❖ A first aid kit

- ❖ A box with a tub of ice cream in it that's full of ice

- ❖ A jumbo packet of crisps

- ❖ A jumbo pack of chocolate

- ❖ A tub of cold ham

- ❖ A mobile phone, iPad and 2 chargers

- ❖ A tub of cold potatoes

- ❖ A box of hot BBQ sausages

- ❖ A bottle of ink

- ❖ A diary

- ❖ Two quills

- ❖ A pack of 100 pieces of paper

- ❖ Packet of chalk

- ❖ Swimming costume x3, clothes, pants, crop tops , PJ's and waterproofs\wellies, and scarf, hat and gloves.

'What is it for, Felicity?' asked Charlie. ' Lily usually forgets stuff. If she has a list if the stuff she brought, when she leaves the place, she can just check the list, and check her rucksack for the stuff that's on the list, then she'll never forget to bring them!' replied Felicity. 'Oh yeah, nice thinking!' said Emily. Suddenly, they heard a noise. At first, they thought it was Miss Nott, but then Emily realized that it was... ' Rachel! Rachel's arrived!' and Emily was right. Rachel came in through the trapdoor and said 'Hi! I've packed and all! You guys should really see the view outside from Emily's window, it's beautiful!' they all rushed up the ladder and stared in awe at the beauty outside Emily's window. 'Wow!' said Lily. It indeed was a beautiful sight. It had stopped raining, and everything was completely drenched. The sky was a lovely pale pink and the golden sun had just risen, making the sea deep- blue and golden. Lily took a photo and sent it to Emily, Charlie, Felicity and Rachel in their group chat. They usually called it ' BFF'S', but since it was Emily's birthday, Lily had changed it to 'Happy birthday, Em!' . They went back into their secret room so Lily could tell them the rest of the plan. Lily told Charlie, Felicity and Rachel the little bit of the plan she had already told Emily. ' So, now you have to listen, Emily,' said Lily. ' This is the rest of the plan. I know a shortcut. I know how to get to Megahurtz lake in one day. So,' she took out her map and said ' It is risky, and that's why we don't go to school the way that I'm going to tell you all about. So, this is Miss Nott's house. 'We go around the back,' Lily traced her finger round Miss Nott's house on her map, ' and then follow this path,' she pointed at a squiggly line, ' but it's not as easy as that. There are men guarding that place so no one can walk along

that path. It's also a kind-of cliff thingy, and those men are on the path. So, if we don't walk on the *path*, then we can get past those guys. So that's sorted. When w-'
' And *how* exactly are we going to 'not walk on the path'?' interrupted Emily. I'll tell you how later!' snapped Lily. 'Yeah, fine,' grumbled Emily. 'When we get past those guys guarding the cliff-path, we'll be in a campsite. Nobody else will be there, and it'll be nice and quiet. We can then set up a tent. Emily has one so we can borrow that one. We can camp there for... we'll decide how many nights we'll stay there once we're there. When we decide that we should go and find out the Baron's hiding place, we change into our swimming costumes and drink the drink to keep us warm. Then we swim across Megahurtz lake, even though it still will be cold, and we'll be swimming to the other side. It's not very big, so we should be able to get to the other side without drowning because of the cold. I'll tell you the rest of the plan later, because Emily needs to write a letter to Miss Nott to tell her where we've went, so she doesn't call the police about a bunch of lost children. But you need to tell her that we'll be fine,' 'Ok, sounds good to me,' said Emily, and took out a piece of paper, her new quill and her ink bottle, then started to write. Hello Miss Nott. this is Emily here. I know you can't find me or Lily Thomas, Rachel Taylor and Charlie and Felicity Duncan. But don't worry and please DON'T CALL THE POLICE OR ANYTHING LIKE THAT because we have gone to try and catch the Baron. Don't worry about us. We'll come home safely

without a single scratch. I will make sure to look after myself. And when I come back, if Lily's plan works, then the Baron will be in jail! Lots and lots of love from Emmeline Sapphire Grey. xxx P.S if you want to know when we're going to come back, then we'll probably be home by.....

Christmas? P.S. I will really miss you! **Lily wrote a letter to her parents too.** Hey Mum, Dad and Lucy **Lily's Little sister** I know you might be worried about me, but don't, because when I come back, the Baron will be in jail! How cool is that Lucy! I know you will miss me, and I will miss you too, but I'm *pretty* safe because I'm with Em, Charles, Fliss and Rach! Will miss you, Lilyanna Mary Swan Thomas. xxxx   P.S I'll probably be home by Christmas. **Charlie wrote one.** Hey Mum, Dad, baby Max, Big sis Amy and Puppy Harry, I know you'll miss me, but I've not died or disappeared into thin air, so there's no point in telling the police about this. but..........guess where I am??? I'M ON AN AMAZING ADVENTURE TO TRY AND CATCH THE WANTED THIEF, THE BARON! Lots of love, Charlie Anthony Masen Duncan. xxxxxxxxx ' **Did you really need to exaggerate'** 'Yeah, I did, Felicity, now get on with your letter and ZIP IT!' replied Charlie. 'Fine,' said Felicity, and started her letter. Dear Family, Charlie has already written you a letter about this, so I am adding on to it. We are indeed going on an expedition to try and put that thief 'the Baron' into prison. Will miss you dearly, Felicity Rose Emerald Duncan. xxxxx P.S we are probably going to come back …..Christmas? **Finally, Rachel wrote her letter. *Hi mum and dad, I am away and trying to catch the Baron. You know, that criminal that's on the loose?***

Don't bother to call the police. I'm going with Felicity Rose Emerald Duncan, Charlie Anthony Masen Duncan, Lilyanna Mary Swan Thomas and Emmeline Sapphire Grey. Will miss you, Rachelina Amythest Daisy Jean Polly Forrest Sedgewick Taylor. xxx 'Wow, you've got a really long name,' said Lily. ' I know,' answered Rachel. 'Right! Now I need to just tell Poppy something,' said Lily, taking everyone's letters. She climbed up the ladder and woke Poppy up once more. 'Poppy, I want you to send these to Charlie and Felicity's house and mine, leave this one here,' she pointed at the one in Emily's handwriting, 'and the third one to Rachel. When you have delivered them, when you come back we will be gone. When Miss Nott wakes up, bark as loud as you can and give her this letter. Understood?' Poppy nodded and barked. Lily gave her the letters, and she held them firmly in her mouth. 'Now, on you go!' Lily said, after she had lowered Poppy in her bucket. Poppy ran off. The sky was slowly turning from pink to blue, and Lily knew that they had to hurry. They pulled on their rucksacks after Emily had packed her's, Lily scribbled on everyone's hands with chalk until they were completely white and then they slowly slid down the pipe. When they reached the bottom of the pipe, they followed Lily's map around the back of the house, before coming to a hault right in front of a path. Well, it wasn't exactly a path, but a sort-of path. It was more a bridge. The bridgey-path was made of white stone and was very wide. It was also *slightly* curved. On the both sides of it, there were extremely deep ditches, which were filled with water which looked...warm. Even though it was a cold winter morning. Emily walked up to the water and touched it. It *was* warm. 'So how are we going-' ' Swim,' replied Lily. 'But-' 'Swim!' repeated Lily, ' and FAST!' ' But-' 'NO BUTS, EMILY GREY! JUST SWIM!' thundered Lily. She ran up to the water and leaped off the edge and landed in it with a splash. Emily thought Lily had drowned, but just then her head appeared, swam up to her, took her hand and pulled her into the warm water. Before Emily knew what was happening, she was already submerged in warm water. ' OH, C'MON GUYS, DON'T YOU KNOW WHAT'S HAPPENING? THOSE GUARDS FOUND US!' now Lily was yelling at Charlie, Felicity and Rachel. They looked behind them, and saw that Lily was right. They ran up to the water and jumped in too. Soon all five of the friends were swimming across the ditch full of water. The guards chased them, but they needed a boat first. So they went and got their boat, and then went back to the bridgy-path, and by the time they had got back the friends were already across. They hadn't managed to catch them, but they knew those five friends were trying to catch The Baron, and whoever tried to catch The Baron never lasted long. The five friends reached the campsite and put up their tent. They had a really fun day. They played hide and seek and tag, they went fishing in Megahurtz lake, cooked the fish and ate it with the roast potatoes. Then it started snowing so they went back in the tent, put their waterproofs on and went back out to play in the snow. They played snowball fights, made snowmen and made snow angels. They played in the snow until 7:00, and then went back inside to have dinner. They had hot barbeque sausages with cold roast potatoes. They went outside once more, and gazed up at the stars, and Felicity used a map of the stars her Grandad gave her. She showed them all the shapes of the stars and told them the legends all about them. Emily's favourite was the tale of Pegasus, the flying horse who helped the Greek hero, Bellerophon defeat the Chimera. They roasted marshmallows over a fire, changed onto their pyjamas and went to bed. It was a bit uncomfortable in their sleeping bags, because the ground was rocky beneath the tent.

CHAPTER 3- THE BARON

Emily woke up early in the morning and saw a little soggy note on the ground. Hi. Just went out to... you know, have a "look" at Megahurtz. See you when I come back. Already had a big dose of "warming drink", don't worry about me. See you soon, Lil x. 'No, Lily, no!' muttered Emily. She didn't want Charlie, Rachel and Felicity to be worried that she'd disappeared, so she wrote a quick note. Hey guys, Lily went to 'look' at Megahurtz, going out to get her. If you wake up early, then help me! Emily. xxx She carefully put Lily's note on top of her's and folded it up neatly. She wrote URGENT in large letters at the front, then slipped it under her pillow. She had no time to change, so she pulled her coat and wellies on, and tore through the forest. At the other side, there was a stony beach, where Emily found Lily's rucksack lying on a large rock, with clothes hanging out of it. She ran down the beach, her legs aching with all that running, until she arrived at the rucksack. Inside was a small note. Emily unfolded it, wondering why Lily had written another note. Hey, water's pretty warm, so I have decided to stay in the water and wait for you guys to come over. We're swimming across Megahurtz TODAY. Lil. xxx Emily stuffed the note back in the rucksack and dragged herself towards Megahurtz. She took off her boots and waded into the water. It was *not* warm. It was absolutely freezing. She walked deeper into the lake until her toes couldn't touch the ground. She wanted to find Lily...but what if she was underwater?

She *had* brought goggles, after all. Emily really hoped the water wasn't salty. She swam a little bit, then ducked her head under the water. She tried to scream as the icy water hit her face, but she was underwater her scream was muffled. Emily opened her eyes. She had never opened her eyes underwater without goggles before, and the water stung her eyes. She looked around her. The water in the lake was a murky greenish- grey colour, and everything was blurry. Emily swam as much as she could, before swimming up to the surface to have a nice, big gulp of fresh air. As her head broke through the water, the cold winter air around her was like summer compared to the ice-cold water she was swimming in. She looked over at the surface-and saw a tired-looking Felicity standing on the shore with her swimming suit on. Emily waved at her, but Felicity didn't wave back. She simply dived into the water and swam up to her. ' We need to find Lily,' said Felicity seriously. ' Yes,' said Emily, and sank back beneath the waves and opened her eyes. Her eyes didn't sting anymore, now that she was used to opening her eyes underwater. Felicity swam alongside her, and after what felt like just minutes, they found Lily. It was quite easy to find her, because she was splashing around madly, trying to float, and gasping for breath. ' I'm s-so s-sorry!' gasped Lily. ' It's alright, we just need to get you out of here!' said Felicity. 'C'mon, take my hand, and Emily's, we'll pull you.' Lily grasped Felicity and Emily's hand firmly, and Felicity and Emily kicked as hard as they could. Gradually, they sped up. Soon they arrived at the shore, where they met Charlie and Rachel, who both had their swimming suits on, and they had packed everything. ' Thanks for being helpful for once, Charlie,' mumbled Felicity. 'Go change, Emily,' she added, handing Emily her swimming suit. ' And *you*,' said Felicity, turning to Lily, ' Are going to wear your spare swimming costume, and so will I.' They all changed, then swung their waterproof bag packs on their backs, and waded into the lake after having a shot of the 'warming drink'. About halfway across the lake, they all started shivering. 'This warming drink isn't as good as a pepper up potion, is it? ' panted Lily, swimming faster than the others. 'Yeah, it would be much better to have a pepper up potion, with steam pouring out of your ears, and being all toasty and warm even though it's really cold. I really wish magic was real.' sighed Emily. 'I definitely agree,' said Felicity.   They kept on swimming until they got to the other side of Megahurtz. They changed into dry clothes and looked around. Right in front of them, there was a giant sign which said: **Beware! This is the Baron's den. P.S you have been warned. The Baron is the most dangerous criminal alive. If you have got to this point, you are lucky to even have SURVIVED. SAY HELLO TO DEATH, and goodbye to LIFE. Its not wise to enter, but if you like you are most WELCOME.** 'I was right! This *is* the Baron's den!' exclaimed Lily excitedly. 'I don't think that's really safe to enter... I'm not sure about this anymore, Lily,' said Emily. 'First you nearly drowned in a freezing lake, and now you want to go into the most dangerous criminal alive's den? You're mad, Lily Thomas!' said Felicity, shocked. 'Well, if you don't want to stop The Baron and be called a hero for the rest of your life, then don't stick with the plan!' said Lily, walking past the sign. Then she disappeared. 'Lily!' cried Felicity, ' I told you not to go!' she stumbled and tripped. She disappeared just like Lily. 'Whenever they land on that spot there, they disappear! It must be a portal! ' said Rachel. 'Yeah, I guess you're right,' said Charlie, not paying attention. Emily kicked him hard in the shins. 'Ow!' he said, rubbing his shins. ' No need to kick that hard! Well, you are right about the portal thing, I suppose,' ' Then come on! Let's get through the portal and help Lily and Felicity!' said Rachel, running forwards and disappearing. Charlie put his hands in his pockets and walked forwards until he too disappeared. Now Emily was standing there alone. She looked back at the sign. They had got so far, this was no time to give up! She sighed deeply, wondering if she'd ever see broad daylight again, ran forwards as fast as she could, and disappeared. It was a horrible feeling, traveling by portal. Emily felt herself falling into complete nothingness. She finally felt her feet hit what felt like a cushion- ground, and then two cold metal walls were squeezing her, and then she was spinning, faster and faster... until her feet hit solid ground. It was light all around her. There was a door and a note from Lily, Felicity , Charlie and Rachel. Hey Em, we went through this door. Once you're in DON'T STEP FORWARD FIVE STRIDES, there are lasers. Yes, Lily is right, and we're going to try and find a way to get past them, or somehow turn them off. *Hi Emily, we were thinking of waiting for you, but we didn't. we decided to catch up with the others.* They told us to write a note to you (with them). *See you soon, Charlie,* **Rachel,** *Felicity and Lil.* xxx Emily tore through the door and found another very small crumpled up piece of paper on the floor. She picked it up. Why did her friends have to write her another note? But she didn't recognise the handwriting. It was neat and swirly. *Whoever dares to take one step into MY lair will die. The Baron.* Emily tore the piece of paper up, and threw it on the ground, then looked around her. All her friends were right. It was very secure indeed. The room was made of metal, and on both sides of Emily were doors. One had a lock on it, and one was wide open. Right in front of her were lasers, and on the other side was a door with a lock on it. Emily went through the open door. She was now in a dimly lit room with only one candle burning low for light. The room smelt strongly of shoe polish, and Emily could taste something rotten. She wrinkled her nose, making her freckles join. The room was full of junk, and Emily could just make out four figures. She squinted at them, and realized they were Charlie, Felicity, Rachel and Lily. Emily took her torch out of her rucksack and flicked the switch from OFF to ON.

Emily blinked, and looked at Lily. Lily was staring back. Then she smiled. ' Come help us find something to get us past the lasers,' she said. Emily nodded, and started to search some boxes tucked into a corner of the room. 'I've found something!' declared Charlie. 'What?' asked Felicity. ' I don't really know. Please can you point your torch in the direction of me, Emily?' asked Charlie. 'Yeah,' said Emily, and turned towards Charlie. He had a flat thing in his hands. 'I think you just found something to fly in, over the lasers! Nice!' said Lily. Charlie carried it out of the room and put it down in front of the lasers. Everybody clambered on, and Lily pushed a shiny blue button. The board rose into the air and soared over the lasers. It landed gently on the ground, and the five friends hopped out. 'Got anymore, Felicity?' asked Lily, holding out her hand. ' Anymore what?' asked Emily. 'Hairpins. The lock on the door was so strong it snapped my hairpin, but still opened the door. Lily, I do have more, but it's my last one. If this lock's too strong, and if it snaps again, then we don't have anymore!' said Felicity, patting her hair for more hairpins. She took it out of her hair and handed it to Lily. The lock was easy to pick this time. With a little *click*, the door swung open. The room was completely different from the last. It was like a house. ' I wonder how the Baron built this,' muttered Lily. 'with the amount of impossible murders, he's done, it seems easy to build this,' said Rachel, gazing around the room. There was a fire crackling merrily in a fireplace in one corner, and in front of the fireplace was a comfy looking couch. There were lots of books; but not ordinary ones. They had titles like How to steal the crown gems or a Beginner's guide to becoming a criminal. Above the fireplace there was a 90-inch plasma TV, and there were four doors on either side of the room which must be the bathroom, kitchen, bedroom and...? They entered the kitchen, stole some snacks, and ate them. They feasted on: chocolate biscuits, wispa gold bars, ready salted crisps (' They're too plain,' groaned Lily) and mozzarella sticks. They put all their stuff in the tumble dryer. Then they went to the bathroom, where they took turns to take a shower, took their dry stuff out of the tumble dryer and went to explore the mystery room. It was filled to the brim with gold! Suddenly, they heard a deep rumbling sound. 'What's that?' panicked Felicity. They could feel the ground vibrating beneath them, and suddenly, it cracked open. They fell about 5 meters and hit a hard-stone floor. 'Is everyone alright?' shouted Emily through the darkness. 'Yeah, but I got a really deep cut right down my arm, said Charlie grimly. He tied one of his t-shirts round it. 'There! Easy!' 'Right, ok, so, let's go on!' Emily could just make out the short figure of Lily. Her face started to glow. ' There's no time to do a TikTok of this, Lily!' cried Felicity. 'I'm not!' her phone torch flickered to life, and she then said, 'Put any kind of light device you have on!' they all obeyed her. Soon there was light filling the corridor. Then they all turned to Lily. 'what next? This was your idea, you should know what to do next!' said Rachel, putting her hands on her hips. Lily hesitated and looked around. 'I think we should search these rooms,' she said pointing to her right. There was a row of doors. Each one had a label. There was: Art Room, Murder Room, Planning Room, Torturing Room, Spying Room and Prison Cell. They searched each room, with no sign of the Baron until... they came to the planning room. It was locked from the inside so they couldn't pick the lock, and without telling anyone, Lily hammered on the door. 'Lily, what are you-' the door creaked open. 'Martin, is that you with my tea?' asked a young man with an oily voice, much oilier than Professor Facts'. He had smooth black hair and icy blue eyes, and when he spotted the children, he twisted his face into a sly grin. It was the most unpleasant thing the children had seen in their lives. 'Well, hello, kids. I'm glad you made it this far… but, I know that young Emmeline Sapphire Grey here has read my note…' 'what note? And how do *you* know Emily's name, and what she did?' ' I have security cameras, and a face scanner, Lilyanna Mary Swan Thomas,' answered The Baron, 'and I was prepared for your arrival, and I know all of your personal information… Emmeline Sapphire Grey, in care of Septima Brazilia Nott, attends Hillton boarding school, has 0 boyfriends… what a pity… ' ' why would you know if I had any *boyfriends?*' 'To kill them, silly girl, but now I have no intention of killing your boyfriends and , for you, dear boy, girlfriends… I want to kill *you*.' He took out a gun just as Emily reached into her rucksack for her phone to call the police. Emily froze. The bang of the gun echoed off the walls. Emily screamed and ducked. The bullet hit her arm, and there was the sound of a bone breaking. Lily ran up to her.   'Are you alright, Emily?' 'Yeah, I'm fine, thanks for asking,' Emily looked shaken, but at least she was alive. The Baron picked them all up by the collars, and threw them out of the room, along with the gun. Then he stalked away. They had to get out of The Baron's den. The girls ran ahead, but Charlie stood still. He wanted to do something first… ' Come on, Charlie!' cried Felicity. 'Yeah, I'm coming!' Charlie zipped up his rucksack, swung it on his back, and ran after them. 'Now how are we going to get out of here?' asked Rachel. She was the tallest, so she touched the tips of her fingers on the cold stone floor on top of them. Nothing happened. 'Maybe there's some kind of secret code,' said Lily. She had a faraway expression on her face. ' Something the Baron likes...' she turned to the doors. Something flashed through her head when she looked at the art room. She trawled through her memories... ' *the Mona Lisa, the most famous painting in the world... any criminal would want to have it, it's worth lots.'.* Any criminal would want to have it! Well say... *the Baron!* 'Mona Lisa,' said Lily confidently. The floor cracked open. 'How did you know that?' asked Emily. 'Common knowledge,' replied Lily. They ran out of the Baron's den and shivered. It was even colder than swimming in the lake. They cleaned up the blood on Emily's arm and placed it gently in a sling. The snow was ankle deep, and the lake was frozen; the ice was thick enough to go skating in. Lily opened her rucksack and wrapped a scarf around her neck. Then her phone gave a loud ring. When Lily ignored it, Charlie made a grab for it in her pocket. Lily tried to fend him off, but he was too tall and quick. Lily accidently pushed Charlie, and he went flying in the air, did a backflip, and landed on the icy lake. 'Ow! I already have a big fat cut here; can't you see that?' He said, rubbing his elbow. He held up Lily's phone triumphantly, unlocked it and read.

41

CHAPTER 4- BACK HOME

Oh, lil, bad, bad lil! I am mising u so! I've sent u a leter but Im wundering how it ll reech u, al the way out ther. U could seereeusly DYE. Oh, why did u go? If u had to, then u coodve taken me to dye with u! I'm soooo angry with u, sis. c u nevur agen, Lucy xxxxxxxxxxxxxx 'You got a message from Lucy,' said Emily, feeling sorry for everyone she'd left behind. 'You've also got a much angrier one from your mum and dad. Your mum was so angry with you she has a lot of spelling mistakes in hers.' said Charlie grimly. 'Here's your dad's.' LILY THOMAS, YOU BAD, BAD, GIRL!!! LUCY IS OH SO SAD, AND YOUR MOTHER AND I ARE MORTIFIED!! The second one said LILIANNA MARY SWAN THOMAS!I MISS TOU DEARTLY. '*What* does the second one say?' asked Rachel. Felicity grabbed the phone off Charlie. 'I think it says… " Lilyanna Mary Swan Thomas! I miss… you dearly.' 'We probably all have messages from our parents to say how bad we are to go along by ourselves. We were so very bad, we shouldn't have listened to Lily.' said Emily, sneering at Lily. ' Then go back to your houses, you silly little goody-goody babies,' spat Lily, turning away from them and ice skating on the lake with her normal shoes on. She played ice-hockey and could ice skate in any kind of shoes. 'C'mon, let's go home,' mumbled Emily, pushing them onto the lake. They put their ice skates on and slid across the lake and descended towards the forest. they reached the campsite and raced towards the bridgy-path. The guards didn't take any notice of them this time, because they thought Lily was dead. Instead they smiled triumphantly at them as they raced towards their homes. Felicity secretly wanted Lily's plan to work, so while she and Charlie were running home, she hid behind some bins and called the police. 'Hello?' said a gruff male voice. 'Hello, Sir. You might recognize the name. f-Felicity. Felicity Rose Emerald Duncan, elder sibling of Charlie Anthony Masen Duncan, Maximus Anthony Masen Duncan, younger sibling of Amy Rose Emerald Duncan and kin of actors Elaine Rose Emerald Duncan and Edward Anthony Masen Duncan.' 'Yeah, I know your parents, alright. Elaine was the main character in my favourite horror film, The night of murders. And your dad was in my favorite thriller, The Spies. Oh, yes, there ain't no actors like your mum and dad,' he chuckled. A pause. 'So, why do you call us so?' ' I think me and my friends just ran into the Baron's den,' she said quietly. 'And I know how to get in.' she explained everything to him, from going across the bridgey -path to running away from The Baron. The police officer listened carefully then said, 'Wow. That's quite an adventure you've had, Miss Duncan. What messages have your parents sent you?' Felicity unlocked her phone and read the messages: Felicity rose emerald Duncan! What a daring girl you are! I heard that you left Lily behind, Charlie told me. He also asked, " where is Fliss? Is she already back home? Maybe she took a wrong turn in the road? She's not behind me. I traced the route we'd taken. She's nowhere to be seen." I really think you should go back to Charlie,

43

and gather your friends, just to go back for Lily. You don't know what danger she could be in, Fliss. I tried calling you- why didn't you pick up? I was worried about you, you. I tried to assure your mother, but she is very frightened. I've used poppy to send you a small letter from mum and I. She should be where you are any minute now. The second said: Dear, oh, dear! Felicity read the first one aloud to the police officer, and he said, 'Hmm-' 'Sorry, officer! I just got a new message!' Felicity opened it excitedly and read it. *Dear Fliss, dad and mum here. We are going to give you short message.* **Just to let you know how we feel about you going off on your own.** *I think you are very brave, but it's not safe and you gave us quite a fright. Young Maxie was so sad. We couldn't sleep for quite a while, he was bawling his tiny little head off. Oh, and by the way, the Baron has been sent to jail. YAY!* **Your father is quite right he was crying, the poor little tyke. Even Amy was crying a little when she came home from shopping for groceries. Please, come home safe.** *Message me back, and your father, please, honey munchkins. Love, Mother and Father.* xxx

Felicity smiled and messaged her mum and dad. Hi mum, dad, Amy and Max (though he doesn't have a phone yet) I'm totally fine. Her mum must have seen that she was typing, because she typed oh, thank goodness! You 're alright! Felicity rolled her eyes. Sometimes her mum could be a little over protective and call her silly names like "little angel" and "baby cakes". I'm coming home right at this moment. She clicked the send button, and off her message went. ' Hello?' Miss Duncan?' she had almost forgotten about the police officer. 'Yes, yes, I'm here.

It was just a quick message from... from my parents. They said people have been sent to arrest the Baron. I-' 'In that case we have it all sorted out! Goodbye, missy!' and he hung up. She sighed and went back to the house. As soon as she went through the door, the loud sound of a baby bawling hit her ears. 'Ow!' she clamped her hands over her ears, muffling the sound. 'Felicity!' it was Charlie. He had a large plaster right down his arm. 'I texted you, didn't you see it? Where were you? Did you go back to Lily, just to say a proper goodbye? Also, we need to go back to her to tell her to come back home because the Baron's been caught fair and square now! Serves him right!' 'No time to answer all these questions, Charlie. But, yes, that was just what I was about to say... we need to, or she might run out of food and die.' Meanwhile, Rachel went back home and was greeted with a welcome home party with lots and lots of hugs and kisses. Emily was not greeted in a nice way at all. She didn't want to. She climbed up the pipe and into the secret room. After a few weeks, she suddenly felt bad for Lily. They had left her behind, abandoned her, let her go out and die... she picked her bag up. She had reached a decision. But she would have to tell Felicity, Charlie and Rachel first... hi. I'm going to go find Lily. U coming? Lily said finally! Changed your mind? Not much signal here, no matter how high up the mountain I go. Can any of u try call? Felicity said well. Me and Charlie were about to do the same... Charlie didn't text anything except yeah. Rachel hurriedly typed yeah, not right now though. I'm in the middle of a welcome home party. Quite fun actually. Pls can u call in… a few minutes? I'll ask if I can be excused. Emily smiled. At least all her friends (even Lily), were still talking to her. Yes, I'm excused from the party. But they said they'd be really strict with me now! Yikes! said Rachel. Emily tapped the call button, and all her friends picked up. Lily's screen was really glitchy, but none of them minded. 'Hi, *crackle*. I'm not sure if you can *crackle* me properly. Can *crackle?*' 'No, Lily, we can't. and your screen's really glitchy.' said Felicity. 'Oh, *crackle. Crackle crackle crackle.*' it was getting worse. Then Rachel had an idea. There was loud music all around her, but her brain was whirring. '*Crackle?*' asked Lily. 'We can't really understand what you're saying, Lily, all we can hear is the wind and crackles,' said Emily. 'What *crackle?*' asked Lily. '*crackle crackle crackle.*' and then she left the call. She tried again. She was higher up on the mountain this time, so her screen was less glitchy. 'I'm bac*crackle!*' 'I know! said Rachel. 'I know how to hear Lily clearly! Don't talk, Lily, switch your camera and microphone off. Get down the mountain and to your bag pack. Text.' '*crackle, crackle!*' said Lily. Then she texted, amazing! Brilliant! Genius! But I don't have a bag pack anymore. ' What? Why?' asked Emily. 'Right, so, you want to go back for Lily,' said Rachel, completely ignoring her. 'Alright! Mum and dad said I can go anywhere now that I've proved I can look after myself! What time to we go to your house? Lily, you're good at planning, you decide!' I think u guys should meet up at Fliss and Charles' house this time. At midnight. K? is everyone alright with that? 'Yeah, Lily, you just wait at your mountain. We'll come for you and we'll stick with the plan!' said Charlie. A relief! Because I just have 1 little tiny problem. I'm stuck on the mountain! I can't get down! I used to though, u know, be able to get up and down the mountain. 'Great,' said Felicity, ' Just great. Are you on the mountain that you told us was a suspicious place?' What do you think? 'Is that a yes?' yeah, obviously. I'm still mad at u guys for abandoning me. I've had quite the adventure already. The lake cracked, I have hypothermia and I lost all my stuff. My rucksack sank to the bottom, and my phone was the only thing I managed to save. It got a little wet, but only a little. Thank goodness I can actual call u! 'Well, gosh, that *is* an adventure! And a bad one, at that!' exclaimed Charlie. 'One moment, guys... got a message...' said Felicity. We have caught the baron, Miss Duncan. There are chances he could escape, and catch your friend, Lily. But we've got it all under control at the moment, so it's fine. When are you going to go for Lily, to bring her back to safety? Please inform us when. Felicity grinned, showing all her shiny white teeth. 'What?' asked Charlie, Rachel and Emily together. Lily texted what? Did you get a message from the Queen or something? Share your screen! 'Probably something even better. Guys, I need to tell you something. The whole thing. The truth. I wanted Lily's plan to work, so while we were running back home, I ducked behind some bins and phoned the police. I told them about our adventure we had, and how we found The Barons' den.I told the police officer that the Baron had been caught. He's in jail now, Lily, so I'm not a goody- two shoes, am I?' no, no, I'm sorry about calling u that. But tell me, y

47

did u have to abandon me? 'We didn't want to make parents really upset about what happened.' said Emily, turning pink and staring at her shoes. Well, that's a pathetic excuse, isn't it? So, u guys really are stupid baby goody two shoes.'*We* aren't babies,' said Rachel suddenly. 'There's something I didn't tell you.' she looked sheepish. 'The call was in full flow, I didn't want to tell you that... that...' 'that what?' asked Charlie.   '

Mumwaspregnantandididn'ttellyouguysandwhilewewereawayshegavebirthtoalittl

ebabygirlandboytwinsactuallyandtheyaresocuteandididn'ttellyoui'msosorry.'

said Rachel. 'What?' asked Emily rudely. Rachel inhaled sharply. ' My mum was pregnant and while we were away, she gave birth to twins. A girl and boy... sorry I didn't tell you.' she was staring at her feet. Silence. Then Lily said are u kidding? U didn't have the chance to tell us! The others nodded in agreement.

CHAPTER 5- LILY'S LOOOONG MESSAGE

Rachel stared at her screen. It said Lily Thomas is typing… 'Lily's typing. Usually she's so quick. Why's she taking so long?' asked Charlie. After 4 and a half minutes of Lily typing, she tapped the send button. Her message said well, guys, this is the longest message I've ever sent. That's why it's taking so long. I've not even shortened any words like, you to u or why to y. and after this message I'm leaving the call. There was a beeping sound and on Charlie's screen it said, Lily Thomas has left the call. He went back to reading Lily's message. It's almost midnight, so I would be very glad for you guys to start getting prepared to leave to Felicity Rose Emerald Duncan and Charlie Anthony Masen Duncan's house. If you look, then there are hundreds of mountains. I chose the front row, so I am near Hillton's village. So, anyway, back to telling you about what mountain to look out for. I never knew nature could be quite so neat. The mountains are in really neat rows and I'm in the one right in front of the village. Please bring as much food as you can. There's another thing I didn't tell you about; but it's not bad. Well, mostly. I stole some of the Barons' gems, and jewels. It wasn't bad stealing, I was stealing from someone who steals. Well, actually, that stuff wasn't the Barons. It was the people he stole it from's property. I'll tell you something I found out later. That's really all I wanted to say to you. See you there! Rachel stood up and picked her bag up from the floor. She was going to Felicity and Charlie's house. Emily did the same. They both left the call and hurried over to Miss Nott's limo. 'We can't just drive this thing ourselves,' Emily said, climbing back up the pipe. 'Where are you going?' called Rachel. 'we don't have much of a choice.' Emily's head poked out of the window. 'I'm tricking.... The chauffer, Mr. Paul!' ' Tricking *who*?' no answer. Emily texted Felicity and Charlie. Hi Felicity and Charlie, I have some orders for you. You simply must obey them, or then we can't go back for Lily. Wear your mourning clothes, and pretend Lily's dead. Not to your parents, though, because you know that she's still alive. But to everyone else, do it. Even me and Rachel. Lie in your beds and pretend you are sad because Lily's died. Tell your parents that you're just pretending, and that you're just playing a silly game, and not to tell anyone that we are "playing". Me and Rachel are going to bring you flowers and cupcakes and cards, and you need to pretend to cry and say thank you at the same time. If you have headache tablets, then put them on your bedside table but DON'T EAT THEM BECAUSE YOU DO NOT REALLY have a headache. Put a glass of water beside you to. Is that clear? Felicity said yeah. She texted Rachel. I want you to go back home, buy flowers, cupcakes and cards, and sign them. Dress in your mourning clothes and come to Miss Nott's house. Pretend Felicity and Charlie are sad and that Lily's dead. No buts or ifs. K? Rachel raised an eyebrow. K, she texted, and darted back to her house.   Emily dressed in her fancy mourning clothes (a black frock with dainty embroidery and beautiful big black roses at the bottom with black tan tights and black high heels). She put her hair up in a neat, pretty bun and pinned it up it a few bobby pins and a clip with black roses on it. She was extremely good at imitating other people's voices and handwriting, so she wrote a note with Miss Nott's handwriting on it.

Dear Steven Paul,

I really suggest you please take my darling Emmeline Sapphire Grey with her friend Rachelina Amythest Daisy Jean Polly Forrest Sedgewick Taylor to her friend's house. She has been with them on the adventure splattered all over the news to catch the Baron, but her friends, Felicity Rose Emerald Duncan and Charlie Anthony Masen Duncan have fallen ill, and she longs to see them and send them cards, flowers and cupcakes. They also want to talk. The illness that they have is not spreadable. I have allowed her to have a sleepover with them for a few days.

Your Mistress, Miss Septima Brazilia Nott.

She folded it up daintily and took out a black handkerchief. She dabbed her eyes a little with it and popped the letter in an envelope. In Miss Nott's loopy, swirly handwriting, she wrote *For Steven Paul , my faithful chauffer.* she went over to his bedroom, and prodded him gently on the shoulder, knowing that he was a very light sleeper. He jerked his body in her direction and looked up at her. 'Oh, Emmeline, you gave me a fright there,' he said, sitting up awkwardly. 'What is it that you want?' Emily burst into tears. 'Oh, whatever's the matter?' he asked. 'And why on earth are you wearing your mourning clothes?' 'Oh, Steven, my best friend Lily died!' she sobbed. 'And here's a letter for you from Miss Nott.' he read it, and then looked up at her sadly. 'Oh, I'm so sorry for you, Emmeline. You must be so sad.' between her sobs, Emily smirked. Her plan was working! He went over to his typewriter and sat down on an old-fashioned stool. The chauffer really liked old-fashioned things. He typed a letter to Miss Nott. He signed it with a flourish and handed it to Emily. She read it. it said:

For Miss Septima Brazilia Nott,

I shall certainly take Emmeline Sapphire Grey and her friend Rachelina Amythest Daisy Jean Polly Forrest Sedgeick Taylor to their friend's house, but I shall have to pay a fine of £80 because the police haven't yet said that you can go out. I don't mind taking the kids to the funeral of their friend Lilyanna Mary Swan Thomas and to visit their other friends Felicity Rose Emerald Duncan and Charlie Anthony Masen Duncan. Anyways, I will always remain your

52

loyal and faithful chauffer, Steven
Paul. *Steven. P*

Emily rushed back into her room and immediately set
to writing another letter.

Oh, Steven Paul,

What a loyal and faithful servant you are! You even are prepared to
break the law in order to fulfill my wishes! The law is no longer there
because The Barn is safe in jail! Thank you, oh, thank you for
saying yes to taking them out!

Your Mistress, Miss Septima Brazilia Nott.

She went back to Steven's room, and he read the
note. He wrote a short note to 'Miss Nott' saying

For Miss Septima Brazilia Nott,

Why, thank you!

Your lovely chauffer, Steven Paul.
Steven. P

Emily smiled through fake sniffs and whispered,
'Thank you so much, Mr. Paul. You're so kind. You
could get murdered by the Baron's gang, yet you are
still taking me and Rachel. Thank you.' ' Why, you're
welcome,' he said gently. Emily felt really bad for
tricking him into driving her and Rachel to Felicity and
Charlie's house, even if it was for a really good reason.
'Well, why don't you go to your room and get your
bag and coat? It sure is cold out, isn't it?' ' Yes.' she
walked gracefully out of the room and up the stairs.
Mr. Paul put his worn leather black jacket on over his

black suit and waited outside the mansion with Rachel. She was wearing a black top and skirt, a black hairband, a black coat, black tan tights and black converses. She had make up on and had smudged it to make it look like she was crying. She was carrying two big bouquets of flowers, home made cupcakes in large containers and two cards which said GET WELL SOON! One was signed by Rachel, and the other one was blank. Emily came out, wearing a black waterproof coat and carrying her rucksack. Rachel gave her the card, and Emily copied Rachel's message.

DEAR Felicity and Charlie,

GET WELL SOON!

I hope that you will start to feel better about life, even after Lily's death.

LOVE FROM, Emily. xxx

CHAPTER 6- RETURN FOR LILY

Tears filled the chauffeurs eyes. He wiped them away with his sleeve and took out the car keys. He opened the door of the car, held out his hand, and helped the two young ladies in, before stepping in himself. He drove them to Charlie and Felicity's mansion and rang the bell. The doorman answered it and stepped aside. The two ladies went inside and up flights of stairs, past rooms and down wide corridors. The walls of Felicity's room had been covered in black washable paint, her bed a pristine shade of black, and on her bedside table there were headache tablets, a box of tissues and a glass of water. The room was completely bare, except for her large oak wardrobe, a desk with loads of note books and pens on it, a large famed picture of Lily on the wall with a garland of flowers around the frame and a bookshelf full of books. On the bed was Felicity, her hair all over the place a crumpled-up tissue in her hand wearing black pajamas and sobbing. She smiled brightly when they came in, tucked a lock of disheveled blonde hair behind her ear and said, ' How do you like it? All my stuff's in the wardrobe. It was big enough to fit almost all my in it stuff in it, including my clothes! The rest is all under here,' she lifted up her bed sheets and pointed under the bed. 'Paint's washable, so once we get to Lily, I'll ask to get it washed off.' she added. 'Brilliant,' breathed Emily 'Absolutely brilliant!' Felicity grinned. 'You should see *Charlie's* room. He always exaggerates things, and I think Charlie's gone way too far with this!' she giggled. They went into Charlie's room. in there was loads and loads of pictures of Lily, and the room was completely bare except his bed. His bedsheets were pristine black, and he was on the bed, sucking on what looked like a headache tablet. ' Charlie, I told you not to eat any of the tablets!' exclaimed Emily. 'Oh, this isn't a tablet,' he said, ' It's a sweet that looks like one.' 'So, you really did exaggerate this,' said Rachel. 'C'mon, let's go get Lily!' 'Um.. We need to go to Felicity's room to do that. She's got a ladder leaning against her window.' he pulled open a loose floorboard and took out his rucksack. Then he went out of the room, Rachel and Emily following. When they got to Felicity's room, she had already combed her long hair, pulled it back in a ponytail, her rucksack on her back and changed into a River Island top and leggings. 'Here,' she said, pulling back her black curtains. They climbed down the ladder as quietly as they could and walked all the way to the bridgey-path. The guards were asleep, so they could get across the bridgey-path without any troubles. They got to the mountain Lily was in, and saw Lily inside, a huddled in a muddy coat, and warming her hands by a fire. She had a few berries beside her and... a tiny tabby kitten asleep by the fire, draped in Lily's scarf. Lily looked up. 'Hi,' she said. ' If you're wondering about her, then here: I found her when I almost drowned. I survived hypothermia, if you were wondering. So anyway, she was the one who saved my phone, and me. I took her in the cave and stole some sweets and crisps. Sorry. I got cat food too, and she's really fun, really. So, then I told her about you guys, and what you look like.' 'Awwww, she's adorable! What's her name, Lily?' said Felicity, stoking her gently. She purred pleasantly. ' Summer,' replied Lily. 'Wow! Summer! And why's that?' said Rachel. 'Well,' Lily blushed, 'I have this *thing* with animals.

'Somehow I know she was born in summer. She's really bright too! And reliable. Whenever you say her name, she comes bounding up to you, and whenever she's cheerful and playful, which is all the time, she begs you for a game. Like, you know, tag, and catch and...' she went on and on about the things they had done. ' I told you that I'd tell you something. It's about the Baron. Charlie...' she looked at him. The others followed her gaze and stared at him. He stood up. 'Well...' he said, shuffling his feet, ' I stole some of the Baron's documents. Don't ask. Here...' he rummaged in his rucksack and took out some papers. 'This is now useless, but I kept them anyway... the Baron's name is not the Baron. It's...' Charlie went pale. 'Michael Edmund Grey, husband of Elizabeth Sapphire Grey and father to.' he swallowed, ' Peter Edmund Grey and... and... *Emmeline Sapphire Grey.*' 'W-what?' stammered Emily. 'The Baron! He's your *father?!* This must be a fake document! No way the Baron is Emily's dad!' 'N-

57

no! that can't be true!' exclaimed Emily. 'M-my parents died in the fire... in our house. We used to live in a manor, and by accident the cook set it on fire! I managed to save a few of my belongings: this locket,' she showed them an expensive looking gold locket encrusted with sapphires, amethysts and rubies 'which has a key to my inheritance and a photo of my parents, and my brother, Pete, I used to call him. He died in the fire along with my parents. I also saved my teddy, that Victorian one, because I was holding it. The rest of my family, some of the servants, and the rest of my belongings burned. Or so I thought. If the Baron is really my father, then one of my relatives that I know are still alive.' ' Why didn't you tell us all this, Emily?' asked Felicity softly. 'My family is famous and were billionaires. It's kind of embarrassing.' 'Wellllll... it doesn't matter now. You've told us now... no big deal!" said Lily, now stroking summer. Summer was blinking her dark eyes at Emily and purring. 'I think we'd better go now,' said Rachel, standing up and starting out of the cave. 'Wait, no!' said Charlie, grabbing her coat. ' I want Emily to do something first. Show us the picture of your father in your locket. Please.' 'Alright,' said Emily airily. 'Here.' she showed them a small picture of: a woman with deep blue eyes and red hair, a man with a gaunt face , black hair and icy blue eyes, a boy, about nine years old, with red hair and icy blue eyes and a tiny girl toddler, about two years old, with wide deep brown eyes. There were the words *The Grey Family* at the bottom.' So the Baron really is your dad,' said Lily. 'where did you get brown eyes from?' asked Rachel, staring into Emily's

58

big brown eyes. 'My gran,' replied Emily. ' Mum's mum.' '*Now* can we go, Charlie?' asked Rachel. 'Yeah,' said Charlie sulkily. 'C'mon.' they all stood up and walked out of the cave. It was surprisingly warm for a winter night, but there was still some kind of wrongness in the air that chilled Emily to the bone. Her flame-red hair was flying out behind her as she walked towards home. When they got to a little graveyard, they saw the Baron there, next to a copper memorial plague. Carved into the copper were the words:

IN LOVING MEMORY OF- ELIZABETH SAPPHIRE GREY:1975-2009

GONE BUT NOT FORGOTTEN

The Baron was writing something else on the grave:

Oh, my dear Eliza, I have found my true daughter, our very own, Emmeline Sapphire Grey. But trying to find her has caused me to do a great sin. I have killed many families, questioning them and demanding answers. I almost killed her, but then realized, after she was gone, that she in my own true daughter. Oh, will you ever find it in your big, warm non-beating heart to forgive me? I miss you dearly. Your husband, Michael Edmund Grey.

' D-dad?' said Emily, appearing out of the shadows. 'Emmeline?' he ran up to her and hugged her tight. 'How do you know I am your father? I escaped from jail just for you!' Emily, startled, slowly wrapped her arms around her father. Then she pushed him away. ' You did a very wrong thing.' she said firmly. 'I know, I know. I deserve to die.' ' Arms up! Oi, you, Baron!

59

Back to jail! Wait a minute... you! You're Emmeline Sapphire Grey, aren't ya? Get away!' 'No, no! he's my father! He didn't mean to kill all of those people!' Men from the army were surrounding them. 'Didn't ya hear me, girl? I said, *get away!*' he's a killer! He might be pretending to be your daddy!' A man with scars covering his face grabbed her roughly by the arm and dragged her away. Emily's heart leaped to her mouth. What was the man going to do to her? 'No! I'm not lying!' cried Emily angrily, digging her nails into the man's rough skin. 'Look!' she opened her locket and showed them all the picture of their family. 'That's dad!' she said, jabbing her finger at her dad in the picture. 'Michael Edmund Grey! Husband of Elizabeth Sapphire Grey and father to Peter Edmund Grey and E m m e l i n e   S a p p h i r e   G r e y.' She said her name slowly. ' Which is me.' 'Oh... then in that case we'll not *kill* 'im, but we'll... we'll... send 'I'm to jail again. And put extra guards!' said the man. Emily went back to her dad. ' Don't try to escape this time, ok? I'll write. Or text. What's your phone number?' ' Look,' he said pulling out his phone. Emily read it and added her father to her chats. His profile picture was the one in the locket, and the group's name was Emily on the Baron's phone, and dad on Emily's. 'Here.' said Michael, offering his hands to a man with an eye patch. He bound them tightly in chains and led him away. It was silent for a few moments, before Charlie, Rachel, Felicity and Lily peeped out from behind the grave where they were hiding. 'That was bloody brilliant,' said Charlie. Emily smiled sadly and texted her first message to her dad: hi, dad, I miss u already. Hope they don't treat u too bad in jail. But I kind of think you deserved it. She sent it. Almost immediately her dad replied: I really miss you too. I'm so very sorry that I killed all those people. Emily smiled and said to her friends, 'C'mon. Let's get home,' and set off. They managed to sneak past the guards on the bridgey-path by hiding in the shadows, and they crept past Mia and Max's house, and to their own houses. There, Lily was given a doctor's care, and Emily got her arm properly cared for. Each family had a joint welcome home party in Felicity and Charlie's house in their disco room and swimming pool in the morning. The rest of the Baron's gang was sent to jail, and the whole of London had a big party because they were free from the clutches of the Baron and his gang. When they got back to school, lots of people started noticing them. Lily smiled shyly, which was very un-Lily-like. They were glad everyone was so happy.

EPILOGUE

'Hey, Happy Halloween, you guys,' said Sapphire, the new American girl with perfectly curled blonde hair, tanned skin and sapphire blue eyes that sparkled. She had made friends with now 16-year old's (and in Charlie and Emily's case, 15-year-old) Charlie, Lily, Emily, Felicity and Rachel. 'Happy all-hallows-eve, Sapphire, 'replied Charlie, picking up a fat slice of pumpkin pie and devouring it. 'This meal sure is delish, innit?' said Sapphire, picking up a sweet in the shape of fangs and sucking on it. 'Looking forward to the disco?' asked Felicity, smiling brightly. ' Yeah, but I like trick or treating better,' said Sapphire. 'Me too!' exclaimed Lily. 'I think we all like trick or treating better,' said Felicity. 'Hey, I've had this type of candy before!' exclaimed Sapphire. 'I had this back home last Halloween!' 'Oh, did you now, little miss I-think-I'm-so-pretty?' asked Sheila, anther new girl who was very plump with a high forehead. She looked a lot like a pig. 'Shut up, Sheila,' said Lily. 'You can't tell me what to do, green-eyed-toad,' said Sheila, her small piggy eyes boring into Lily's green ones. 'I said *shut up* Sheila,' said Lily. Sheila went bright red, and slapped Lily hard, right across the face. Lily slapped her back, harder. Sheila wrestled her to the ground, clawing at her face. Lily tried desperately to fend her off, but Sheila was too fat and tall. 'Stop, stop, just stop!' cried Sapphire, trying to separate Lily and Sheila, but they were too strong. Sapphire fell backwards. She sighed and went into the sixth-year dormitory to write a letter to her parents, 3 sisters and 4 brothers.

Hey Mom, Dad, Olivia, Emerald, Ruby, Logan, Stewart, Max, and Billy, I really miss you, but it's really fun here, honest. This is the best school you could ever go to. I mean, we celebrate birthdays in our grades, Christmas, it's really REALLY fun, Easter and Halloween, or All-Hallows-Eve, as they call it here. Hope life in LA is alright, and the Wildfires have gone down. Hope you are all safe. I'm am safe over here. There aren't any Wildfires! I'm like OMG! This place is AWESOME! I've already made 5 friends. They're called: Charlie, Felicity, Rachel, Lily and Emily. They're nice. Felicity and Charlie are brother and sister with blonde hair and blue eyes, but not as deep as mine. Rachel has white- blonde hair and blue-green eyes. Lily is a little tanned, (but not as tanned as me), with green eyes and brown hair. Emily has perfectly curled red hair, freckles, braces , brown eyes, and ,like, really pale skin. Like , I mean it's like someone's painted her face white and added the slightest bit of a peachy tinge to her skin. I've made 1 enemy too. She's called Sheila. She always calls me " Little Miss –I-Think-I'm-So-Pretty". Seriously?' There's only one explanation to what she looks like: A Pig. Ha, ha! Lots and Lots of Love, Sapphire Victoria Battersea. xxx

By the time sapphire had posted her letter and came back to the castle, Lily and Sheila had been sent to the headmaster's office. 'Next lesson- swimming,' declared Charlie. 'C'mon, let's go.' 'I heard that instead of a normal swimming lesson, we're having a spooky pool party,' said Sapphire excitedly, as they hurried to the swimming pool room. 'Then you heard right,' said Rachel. ' And I wasn't eavesdropping, but I over-heard a group of first years talking about you going on this adventure to catch a criminal called The

Baron... and you succeeded. Is this true?' she added. Emily blushed. 'Well, yes,' she said, shuffling her feet and looking down at her swimming kit. ' It was four years ago, though. Ages ago... The Baron's in jail, now. He's my dad.' 'Um... what?' Emily took a deep breath. 'He's my dad.' she showed Sapphire her texts to him.

A few weeks later Lily met Sapphire. 'You weren't at trick or treating,' said Sapphire. 'Look, I texted my mom and dad about how much fun I had.' she showed Lily her text: **Hey mom and dad, I had SOOO much fun today! Everything, and I mean, like, EVERYTHING, even lessons, were Halloween themed! E.g. swimming was a spooky pool party, in history we learned about the history of Halloween, All-Hallows Eve, All Saints Day or... Samhain (pronounced sow-in)! It was Awesome! We had a Halloween feast, a disco, and we even went trick or treating! It was SOOOOOOOOO FUN!!!!!** 'Oh, that's so nice. I wish I was there,' said Lily sulkily. 'Oh, well, try not to get into too much trouble at Christmas!' laughed Emily.

The next day, Sapphire got a letter from her family. *Oh, Sapph, we're fine. The wild fires have in fact got worse, but still, we remain safe. This is only because we decided to move nearer to you. Your letter was redirected to us here in the UK - we are now in South Yorkshire. It is really much better here, though we are getting used to the accent. It is so nice that you have made that many friends already. I really look forward to meeting them on Visitors Day. Just try and ignore Sheila. That's the best thing to do. Loads and loads of love, Olivia,* Mom, **Dad**, Emerald, RUBY, Logan, *Stewart,* Max *and* Billy.xxxxxxxx

Sapphire's eyes filled with tears. 'My family have moved to South Yorkshire! They had to leave Los Angeles!' Her make up got smudged as tears hopelessly spilled down her face. 'Oh, it's alright, Sapphire,' said Rachel and Lily together, rushing forward to help. 'I-I'm s-sorry. It-it's just...' 'We understand, Los Angeles was your home, and you are sad it's in wildfires and all that.' said Lily smoothly, as if she had spent the whole of her detention rehearsing it. ' You miss home. You're home-sick.' 'Y-yeah, and all that...' 'Don't worry,' said Charlie firmly. 'I'm sure you'll get your home back soon.'

Printed in Great Britain
by Amazon